SCOTT, FORESMAN SECOND TALKING STORYBOOK BOX

A Ride On High by Candida Palmer

A Time for Flowers by Mark Taylor

Alfred by Janice May Udry

Amigo by Byrd Baylor Schweitzer

April's Kittens by Clare Turlay Newberry

Blaze and the Forest Fire by C. W. Anderson

Cinderella retold by Evelyn Andreas

Felice by Marcia Brown

Fly High, Fly Low by Don Freeman

If I Drove A Truck by Miriam Young

In the Middle of the Night by Aileen Fisher

Lentil by Robert McCloskey

Major, The Story of a Black Bear by Robert M. McClung

Mr. Angelo by Marjory Schwalje

My Dog Is Lost! by Ezra Jack Keats and Pat Cherr

*No Roses for Harry! by Gene Zion

Noisy Nancy Norris by LouAnn Gaeddert

Sam by Ann Herbert Scott

Song of the Swallows by Leo Politi

The Emperor's New Clothes by Hans Christian Andersen

*The Happy Lion by Louise Fatio

The Story of Paul Bunyan by Barbara Emberley

What Do You Say, Dear? by Sesyle Joslin

*Not included in sets for distribution in France or the British Commonwealth (except Canada).

NOISY NANCY NORRIS

By LouAnn Gaeddert
Illustrated by Gioia Fiammenghi

NOISY NANCY
NORRIS

DOUBLEDAY & COMPANY, INC.

GARDEN CITY, NEW YORK

Special Scott, Foresman and Company Edition
for *Scott, Foresman Second Talking Storybook Box*

LIBRARY OF CONGRESS CATALOG CARD NUMBER 65-10180

TEXT COPYRIGHT © 1965 BY LOUANN GAEDDERT

ILLUSTRATIONS COPYRIGHT © 1965 BY GIOIA FIAMMENGHI CAPUTO

ALL RIGHTS RESERVED

PRINTED IN THE UNITED STATES OF AMERICA

This special edition is printed and distributed by
Scott, Foresman and Company by special arrangement with
Doubleday & Company, Inc., Garden City, New York, 11530.

To My Parents
Louis and Louise Bigge

Nancy Norris was a very noisy child.

She liked to ride her stick horse
and pound
the end
of it
on
the
floor.

Nancy
liked
to clomp
down the hall
in her mother's
high-heeled
shoes.

She liked to sit
on the radiator cover and
bang her feet.

She even thumped her clay so that the table jumped.

Sometimes she banged her doll buggy into the walls.

Her pretend games were always noisy. When she was a garbage man, she banged two big pans together, making almost as much noise as a real garbage man.

When she was a fireman,
she made a noise
that sounded like a siren.

14

When she was an elephant, she made great
clattering feet out of her mother's cake pans.

And, of course, she sang and talked most
of the day.

Sometimes, when Nancy had been talking a long time, her mother would say, in a voice louder than Mother usually used, "Please, please be quiet so I can think." Nancy tried to be quiet but it was very difficult.

Nancy lived in an apartment house and

her noises often disturbed the neighbors.

Her friend Sally lived on the floor above
and Nancy used to go to the stairway and

call up to her, but Nancy's mother put a
stop to that.

Mrs. Muffle, who owned the whole build-
ing, lived in the apartment just below the
Norris's. When Nancy hopped down the
hall like a kangaroo, the chandelier in
Mrs. Muffle's hall tinkled.

When Nancy jumped off her bed, there
was a thud over Mrs. Muffle's head.

On days when Nancy was especially noisy, Mrs. Muffle would get a broom and bang on her ceiling so that Nancy would hear the bang on her floor. Nancy thought that was very funny. She would get a block and bang back.

But Nancy's mother would be cross.

"You are disturbing poor Mrs. Muffle," she would say. "Why don't you finger-paint?" But Nancy even made a crackle-slush sound with the paints and paper.

Then came the bad day.
It was raining when Nancy woke up
and she felt cross so she sang,
*"Bad morning to you,
bad morning to you."*
But she didn't really sing, she shouted.
Then she stood on her bed
and jumped to the floor.
While she was getting dressed she dropped
her shoes one after the other.
She slammed the door five times.

She rattled a stick against the wall as she ran down the hall to the kitchen and she scraped her chair out from under the table and knocked it over. While she was eating breakfast, she tapped her spoon on her plate—until her father asked her to stop.

After breakfast, she picked up a waste-
basket and drummed on it while she sang
and marched through the living room.

She was still marching
when the doorbell rang.

Nancy rushed to the door and there was Mrs. Muffle.

"Where are your parents?" she demanded.

Mother and Daddy said, "Good morning," and "How are you?" and all of the polite things that grownups say. Mrs. Muffle didn't answer them. She just glared at Nancy and said, quietly of course, "I've had all the noise I can take. You will have to move unless I have complete peace and quiet from now on."

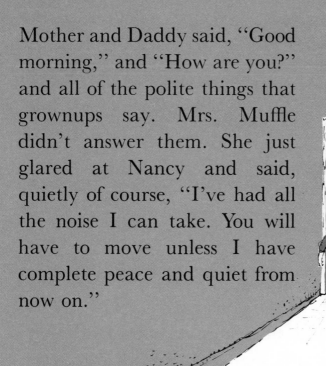

She walked out without saying Good-by.

Nancy and her mother and daddy sat
staring at the door, which closed quietly
behind Mrs. Muffle. "Oh, my," moaned
Mother.

"Did you hear what she said?" asked
Daddy. "I know it will be difficult, Nancy,
but you must be quiet or we will have to
move—away from your friends and your
playground, maybe even out of the city."

Nancy nodded and tiptoed to her room
and sat on the bed.

She was still sitting there,
thinking and doing nothing,
when Daddy came to kiss her good-by
before he went to his office.

Nancy just said, "Good-by" very softly.

Then Mother came to tell her that she was going out and that Grandma would stay with her.

Grandma came and Mother went.

"Come out to the living room and talk with me, Nancy," Grandma called. Nancy went. "How are you, dear?" asked Grandma.

"Fine," she whispered.

"Did you go to the playground yesterday?"

"Yes," said Nancy.

"What did you do?"

"Played," said Nancy.

"Is something the matter?" asked Grandma. "You seem very quiet."

"No," said Nancy.

Grandma read her a story and then Nancy went to her room and looked at picture books.

When Nancy's mother came home, Grandma told her that there was something wrong with Nancy. "I have been here for two hours and she hasn't said more than a few words. She hasn't jumped. She hasn't run."

As soon as Grandma went home, Mother took Nancy's temperature. "No fever," she said. "Do you feel sick?" Nancy shook her head.

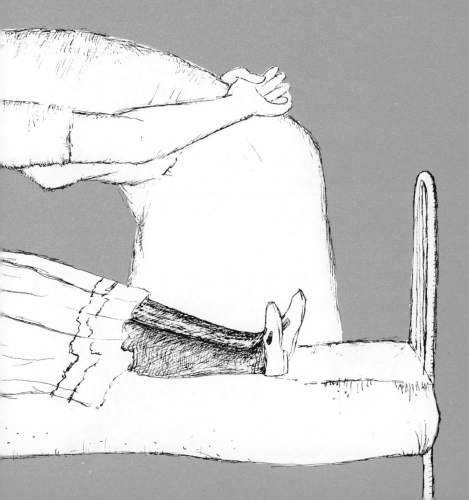

She was quiet all day. She played with her puzzles, but she didn't even click the pieces.

She played elephant but she pretended to be walking silently on long green grass.

She undressed all her dolls and wrapped
them in blankets and put them to bed.

When Daddy came home,
she started to run
down the hall to greet him.
Then she remembered
and tiptoed
the rest
of the
way.

When it was time for dinner, she pulled
her chair out quietly.

"What have you been doing today?"
Daddy asked.

"Playing," said Nancy.

"Did you have fun?"

Nancy nodded. She shrugged her shoulders.

Then Mother and Daddy started talking to each other while Nancy ate everything on her plate.

"My, but you finished quickly," said Daddy
to Nancy.

"That's because she hasn't been talking,"
said Mother.

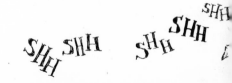

Nancy went to bed quietly. Of course she slept quietly.

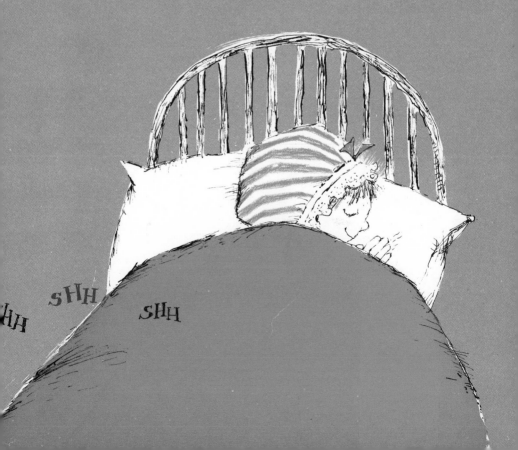

When she woke in the morning she started to sing, "*Good morn . . .*"

But she remembered Mrs. Muffle's visit and she didn't finish.

Later in the morning, Nancy and her
mother went to the playground.

Sally was climbing on the monkey bars. "Hi, Nancy," she shouted. Nancy just waved to her and snuggled closer to her mother. She watched Michael and John playing on the slide.

"Go play with them," said Mother. "And make noise. This is the place for it." Nancy thought a minute, smiled, and made a great "r-r-R-RRR" noise and ran toward the slide.

She climbed to the top,
clanged her feet
and slid down,
bumping into John,
who was sitting
on the bottom.

When Nancy rode on the back of Michael's trike, they pretended it was a fire engine. Nancy made her best siren noises.

Then they played garbage man,
making loud clatters
with their sand pails.

Nancy made noise all morning . . .
and she talked to her mother
all the way home.

But the minute they entered their apartment-house door, she stopped talking and she didn't say a word in the elevator . . . or as they walked down the hall to their door.

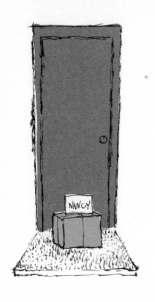

Right in front of their door was a box with an envelope on top with Nancy's name on it. Nancy opened the box.

It was filled with cookies. Mother read the letter to Nancy.

Dear Nancy,

My but it has been quiet down here. Almost too quiet. I hope you're not sick. Please make just a little noise so I'll know you are all right.

Sincerely,

Mrs. Muffle.

Nancy smiled. Then she began to laugh. It would be so much easier to make a little noise than to make no noise at all.

She picked up her stick horse and galloped to her room—remembering not to bang the end of the stick on the floor.

LouAnn Gaeddert has had varied experience in the publishing field, working with both books and newspapers, but this is the first book she has written. As the apartment-dwelling mother of two young children, she has chosen a subject with which she is very familiar.

Mrs. Gaeddert is a graduate of the University of Washington. Seattle is her home town, but she and her family now live in New York City.

Gioia Fiammenghi was born in New York City, and attended various art schools in that city. She has illustrated over twenty books, both for children and adults, and also has paintings on exhibit. She now lives in Monte Carlo, Monaco, with her husband and three young sons.